D0627433

The Twin Giants

For
Mavis

M. G.

This is a work of fiction. Names,
characters, places, and incidents are either
products of the author's imagination or,
if real, are used fictitiously.

Text copyright © 2007 by Dick King-Smith
Illustrations copyright © 2007 by Mini Grey

All rights reserved. No part of this book may be reproduced,
transmitted, or stored in an information retrieval system in any
form or by any means, graphic, electronic, or mechanical, including
photocopying, taping, and recording, without prior written permission
from the printer.

First U.S. edition 2008

Library of Congress Cataloging-in-Publication Data is available.
Library of Congress Catalog Card Number pending
ISBN 978-0-7636-3529-9

2 4 6 8 10 9 7 5 3 1

Printed in Singapore

This book was typeset in Caslon Antique
and Ludovico Woodcut.
The illustrations were done in ink, watercolor,
colored pencil, and digital collage.

Candlewick Press
2067 Massachusetts Avenue
Cambridge, Massachusetts 02140

visit us at www.candlewick.com

The Twin Giants

Dick King-Smith

illustrated by Mini Grey

CANDLEWICK PRESS
CAMBRIDGE, MASSACHUSETTS

Mountain Number 1

The Seven Mountains

Mountain Number One

ONCE UPON A MOUNTAIN, THERE LIVED

two brother giants. Twin brothers, in fact,

something that's rare among giants. When the

first one was born, his giant father looked at

the huge baby and said . . .

1

And when the second one arrived, his giant

mother looked at the huge

baby and said . . .

"There's a-lot-uv-'im!"

And that's how the twin giants got their names.

Time passed, and Lottavim and Normus grew . . .

4

and grew.

5

They loved playing games. They liked races:

Down the Mountain

(Start from the top; first to reach the bottom wins.)

and

Up the Mountain

(Start from the bottom; first to reach the top wins.)

These races were always close, often

dead heats, and the time each race took

6

grew shorter as the giants' legs grew
longer.

They also liked to play a game called Roll
the Boulder. They would choose two gigantic
lumps of rock and put them side by side at the
top of the mountain. Then one or the other
(they took turns) would shout, "Roll!" and each
would give his rock
a shove, and down
the mountainside
the two great lumps
would go bouncing.
The winner was the
one whose boulder
went the farthest.

The other thing that Lottavim and
Normus liked to do was sing. They would sit
side by side inside the cave where they lived,
and sing the songs their giant parents had
taught them — very, very loudly, of course.
This might not have been too bad if either of
them had been able to sing in tune, but neither
could. In the rich and fertile valley below the
mountain, mothers would tell their
naughty children, "Behave
yourselves, or the giants
will get you."

Lottavim and Normus always did everything together. They walked in step with each other. They woke up and went to sleep at exactly the same time. They even sneezed at the same moments.

But the twins

were different

in one way....

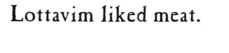

Lottavim liked meat.

Normus liked vegetables.

This had been the case right

from the start. When their parents raided the

farms and market gardens in

the rich and fertile valley below,

they might bring back, say, a

nice spring lamb and a couple dozen young

cabbages, and Lottavim would

always make a grab for the lamb

and Normus would always

lunge for the cabbages.

Now, giants do not live

very long lives, and when the

twins were only twelve years old

and twelve feet high,

both their parents died.

So Lottavim and Normus had

to learn to find their own food. Twice a week,

on Wednesdays and Saturdays, they

would thunder down the

mountainside, each with a

great sack slung over his

shoulder, and make the rounds of

farms and market gardens, and

of dairies and henhouses and

beehives and orchards

(for Lottavim did like fruit and

Normus was rather fond of

milk and eggs and honey).

On those days, the people of the rich
and fertile valley locked themselves in their
houses, all hoping that the giants would steal
someone else's produce.

The brothers had to learn how to cook, too, and how to keep a tidy cave. After a time they got used to it — though each always said to the other, "The one person I couldn't do without is you, Lottavim," or "you, Normus," depending on which one was speaking.

Only when they reached the age of twenty and the height of eighteen feet did Lottavim and Normus stop growing. To look at, if anyone had been brave enough to take a good close look at them (which no one was), they were almost impossible to tell apart. They still did everything at the same time, but now that they were grown, something changed, for both of them.

For a time they did not discuss this change openly, but one evening after supper, when Lottavim had just polished off a baron of beef and Normus was chock-full of chickpeas and cheese and chives, they looked at each other and knew, beyond a shadow of a doubt, just what the other was thinking.

With one breath, they said, "It's about time I found a wife," and the very next morning, they set off.

Mountain Number Two & Mountain Number Three

THERE WERE OF COURSE PLENTY OF GIRLS

of marriageable age in the rich and fertile

valley below, but neither twin was the

least bit interested in such midgets,

mostly less than five and a half feet tall.

19

No, no, what each had in mind was nothing less than the giantess of his dreams.

Giants and giantesses — the brothers had been taught — lived only in the mountains, up or down which they, with their twelve-foot strides, could walk twice as easily as ordinary folk. So Lottavim and Normus wasted no time in the valley behind their home but marched across it, side by side and keeping step, and climbed the mountain beyond.

Near its summit, they met a very old, white-haired giant who said, "Hello. Who are you and what do you want?"

The twins introduced themselves.

"We're each looking for a wife, sir,"

they said politely. "Do you have any daughters?"

"One," said the old giant. "She's out getting my lunch."

Just then they heard a rattle of stones farther down the mountainside and saw a figure coming up the slope. As the figure drew closer, the twins saw that it was a giantess, almost as tall as they were, carrying a dead sheep across her shoulders. With one voice, they said to her, "Will you marry me?"

The giantess gave a giant giggle. "I can't marry both of you!"

"Oh," said Lottavim.

"Oh," said Normus.

"And anyway, I'm afraid I can't marry either of you. I've got to look after my old dad."

"Tough break, boys!" said the old giant with a grin.

As they plunged away down the mountainside with giant strides, Normus said, "I've been thinking, Lot."

"So have I, Norm," said Lottavim, "and I have an idea."

"Me, too," said Normus. "If we do meet any other girls, we'll only be competing against each other."

"Exactly. But if we split up for a while, each of us might find what he's looking for on his own."

"Exactly."

So when they reached the next mountain, each went his separate way: Lottavim up one side and Normus up the other.

It was not long before Lottavim came upon a young giantess sitting on a rock, eating raw green beans. There's no time to waste, he thought, so he said, "Hello and are you married, and if not will you marry me?"

"You move fast," said the giantess. "The answers are — no, I'm not married, and it depends."

"Depends on what?"

"Whether you eat meat."

"Of course I do," said Lottavim.

"In that case," said the giantess, "I'm afraid I wouldn't marry you if you were the last giant on earth. I strongly disapprove of meat eating. I'm a vegetarian."

Wow! thought Lottavim. Just right for my brother. And he hurried away, shouting, "Norm! Norm! Where are you?"

Normus, around the other side of the

mountain, had also come across a young

giantess, who was also sitting on a rock,

except she was gnawing on a beef bone.

"Hello," he said. "I'm looking for a single girl who wants to get married. Any chance you're available?"

"You don't mess around, do you?" she replied. "Yes, I'm available. Have a bit of my bone."

"No, thanks," said Normus. "I'm a vegetarian."

"Oh dear, oh dear," said the giantess. "The giant I marry has to like meat."

Wow! thought Normus. Just right for my brother. And he hurried away, shouting, "Lot! Lot! Where are you?"

When the brothers met up and told each other what had happened, each set off to meet the giantess the other had found. Each now knew that the giantesses were single, so when Lottavim found the beef eater, he started right in.

"Will you marry me?" he said.

"I've already said no," she replied.

"That was my twin brother," said Lottavim. "I'm a meat eater."

"Twin brother!" she said. "Ha, ha, funny joke."

When Normus came upon the bean-eating giantess, he, too, wasted no words and immediately proposed.

"I've already refused you," she said.

"That was my twin brother," said Normus. "I'm a vegetarian."

"Twin brother!" she said. "I've heard that one before."

When the brothers met again, Lottavim said, "I told her I was a meat eater, Norm, but she said no."

"I told her I was a vegetarian, Lot," said Normus, "but she said no."

"Talk about fussy," said Lottavim. "Why can't they be easygoing like us?"

"Exactly," said Normus. "Why can't a giantess be more like a giant?" And side by side and keeping step, they marched away toward the next mountain.

Mountains Number Four, Five, & Six

BUT THOUGH THEY CLIMBED THE NEXT

mountain and searched thoroughly, they found

no giantesses. Nor did they on the fifth

mountain. Nor on the sixth.

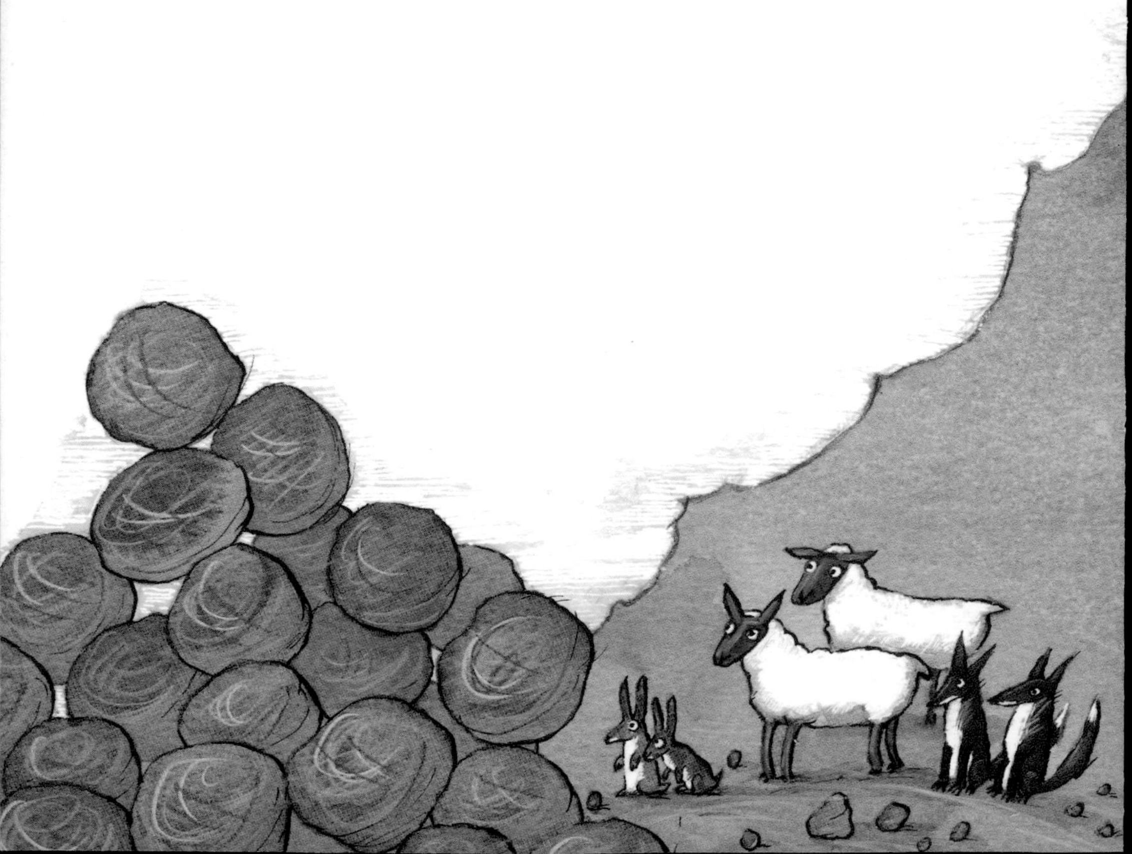

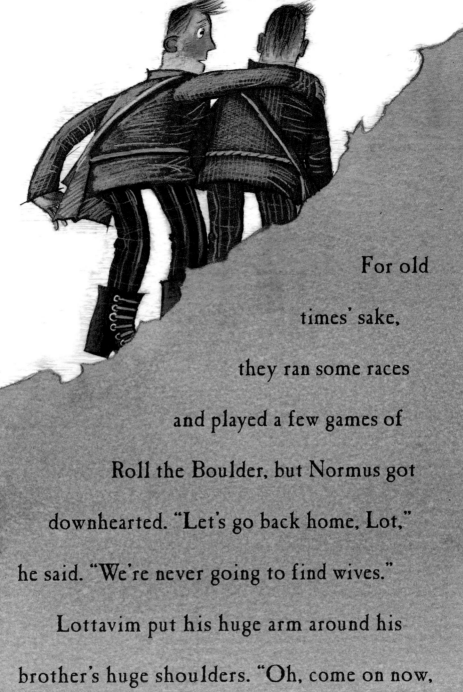

For old
times' sake,
they ran some races
and played a few games of
Roll the Boulder, but Normus got
downhearted. "Let's go back home, Lot,"
he said. "We're never going to find wives."

Lottavim put his huge arm around his
brother's huge shoulders. "Oh, come on now,
Norm," he said. "The next mountain will be
the seventh, and seven's a lucky number."

Mountain Number Seven

"FINGERS CROSSED, NORM," SAID LOTTAVIM

as they reached the foot of the seventh

mountain, and each of them crossed two of

their ten-inch fingers. Then they went their

separate ways up the mountain's steep slopes.

On the eastern side of the mountain, Normus came upon a family of giants. They made him very welcome, offering him a whole suckling pig, which of course he refused, pretending that he had just eaten. But he did accept a small snack of a dozen apples, six pears, and a pumpkin.

There was a mother giant and a father giant and three giant children, all boys.

"Fine sons you have," said Normus to the father when he could get a word in, for they were a talkative lot. "No daughters?"

"No," said the mother.

"You married?" asked the father.

"No," said Normus.

The father and mother looked at each other and smiled.

"Try the other side of the mountain,"

they said.

On the western side, Lottavim was in a daze of happiness. Halfway up, he had paused to rest awhile and was admiring the view below, when he heard steps behind him. He turned to see a giantess. And what a giantess! She was almost as tall as he was—perhaps sixteen and a half feet, and her hair was corn-colored and her eyes sea blue and her teeth pearly white. Lottavim stared at her, dumbstruck.

"Hello," she said in a voice like warm honey. "Who are you?"

Lottavim smiled. "My name is Lottavim," he replied.

"My name," said the beautiful giantess, "is Georgina, but you can call me Georgie if you like. Can I do anything for you?"

Oh yes, thought Lottavim. You can be my wife! This is it! This is the real thing! This is love at first sight!

"Tell me you're not married," he said.

"I'm not," said Georgina.

"Tell me you're not a vegetarian."

"I love all sorts of food."

Lottavim took a deep breath.

"D'you think," he asked,

"that you could love me?"

Georgina burst out laughing. It was a

jolly, bubbly laugh, an infectious laugh, and

Lottavim found himself laughing with her.

"I like you," she said.

They stared at each other, and then

Lottavim reached out and took her huge

hand in his even huger one.

"Georgie," he said.

"Yes, Lottavim?"

"I am looking for a wife."

"Look no further."

"Oh, Georgie!" said Lottavim. "You have

made me the happiest giant in the world!"

Just then they heard a voice calling,

"Lot! Lot! Where are you?"

"Who's that?" asked Georgina.

"My twin brother, Normus."

"Your twin brother?"

"Yes."

"Identical?"

"Yes," said Lottavim. "He's looking for a

wife, too." And then, as Normus came into sight,

"But it doesn't look as though he's had any luck."

"Norm, old boy," he said when his brother reached them, "allow me to introduce Georgina, Georgie for short."

This is it! thought Normus. This is the real thing! This is love at first sight!

"I hope you'll be very happy, Norm," said Lottavim (*We shall! We shall!* thought Normus), "to know that Georgie and I are going to be married."

Normus's jaw dropped.

He stared at the pair of them, speechless. Then, somehow, he managed a smile. Somehow he stammered out words of congratulations. He stood and watched as the happy couple descended the slopes and set off, hand in hand, for home.

For a long time Normus sat there, the picture of misery. *If only I had gone around the western side and Lot around the eastern,* he thought. *Or if only I hadn't spent so much time eating and talking with that family, I still might have met her first. As it is, Lot is to marry the giantess of my dreams. I shall never meet another like her. And what's more, I shall never see my twin* brother again — I couldn't bear to go home

and be the third wheel. Two's company;

three's not. I'm on my own from now on.

He put his giant head in his giant hands

and heaved a giant sigh.

"You don't sound very happy," said a voice suddenly, a voice like warm honey.

Normus raised his head from his hands to see Georgina standing before him, showing her pearly white teeth in a smile, her sea-blue eyes twinkling, her corn-colored hair blowing in the mountain breeze.

She's come back! he thought. She's decided against poor old Lot! She's chosen me instead!

"Oh," he said. "So you're not going to marry Lottavim?"

The giantess looked puzzled.

"Marry who?" she asked.

"Lottavim."

"Certainly not."

Normus swallowed.

"I have to tell you," he said, "that I'm a vegetarian."

"Doesn't worry me."

Normus took a deep breath.

"In that case," he said, "will you marry *me*?"

"I quite like that idea," said the beautiful giantess, "though I haven't a clue who you are."

"I'm Lottavim's brother, Normus. Don't you remember me, Georgie?"

"No," said the giantess, "because I'm not Georgie. I'm Alexandra, though you can call me Alex."

"I don't understand," said Normus. "How can you be so *exactly* like Georgie?"

"Because," replied Alexandra, "she is my identical twin sister."

Mountain Number 1

The SeVeN Mountains

Mountain No TWO

MOUNTAIN 4

Number FIVE

Mountain No. 3

MOUNTAIN number SIX

GIANT MAP Company

MOUNTAIN No. 7

N
W   E
S

Choose a Mountain

EVEN THOUGH BOTH WERE SO MADLY IN

love — Lottavim with Georgie, Normus with

Alex — the twin brothers were thinking, at

exactly the same moment, about each other.

Poor old Norm, thought Lottavim. He'll be so lonely and miserable on his own.

Good old Lot, thought Normus. He'll be so happy to know that I've been as lucky as him.

So when Lottavim said to Georgie, "I must go and find Norm; he'll be so unhappy," she replied, "No need. Just look who's coming." For there, striding hand in hand up the slopes of Mountain Number One, were Normus and Alex.

"How on earth . . . what . . . who . . ." gabbled Lottavim. "She looks exactly like you!"

"She's my twin sister, Alexandra," said Georgie, "and she is like me in every way, except that I'm in love with you and she, by the look of things, is in love with your brother. He doesn't seem to me to be at all unhappy."

What a celebration there was when the two couples met at the cave!

All four roared so long and so loudly
in their delight that the villagers in the rich
and fertile valley below thought that the end
of the world was upon them.

"How happy our father and mother would have been for us," said Lottavim to Normus.

"Would have been?" said Georgie. "You mean . . . ?"

"Yes," said Normus, "they died eight years ago."

"How odd," said the sister giantesses.

"Odd?" said the brother giants.

"Yes, because our parents would have been so happy, too."

"Would have been?" said Lottavim. "You mean . . . ?"

"Yes," said Georgie. "They died two years ago. Alex and I have lived alone in our cave ever since."

There was a silence. The twin brothers looked at each other. "One cave on Mountain Number One . . ." said Normus, and "One cave on Mountain Number Seven . . ." said Lottavim. "Makes one cave for each couple," said Georgie and Alex with one voice. "Who's going where?"

Lottavim took a huge
gold coin from his pocket.

"We'll flip for it, shall we, Norm?" he
said. "Heads—Georgie and I stay here, and
you and Alex go back to the other cave. Tails—

you and Alex stay

here, and Georgie

and I go back."

"All right,"

replied Normus.

I don't care which cave I

live in as long

as my brother

is happy,

he thought.

Lottavim balanced the huge coin on his

huge thumb. I don't care which cave

I live in as long as my brother is happy,

he thought.

I hope it's heads, Georgie thought. I like

this cave.

I hope it's heads, Alex thought.

I'd rather go back home.

"Go on then,

Lot," said Normus,

so Lottavim

flipped the huge

coin with his giant

thumb and it came

down heads.

61

I expect you can guess that, as time went by, there was a great deal of traffic between Mountain Number One and Mountain Number Seven. Life for the villagers in the rich and fertile valley became even more difficult.

At first it was just the two couples of

giants visiting each other, but later Georgina

had babies and Alexandra had babies (on the

same day, of course). I say "babies" because
(would you believe it?) each of the sisters
gave birth to twins!

On that wonderful day, Lottavim

charged down from the cave on Mountain

Number One, singing out in his awful voice,

to tell his brother the glad news, and

Normus charged down from the cave on
Mountain Number Seven, singing out in
his awful voice, to tell his brother the
glad news.

"You'll never guess, Norm!" shouted Lottavim as they met, and "You'll never guess, Lot!" shouted Normus, and then they looked at each other and each somehow knew.

"I've got twins," said Normus in what was, for him, a quite quiet voice. "You, too?"

"Me, too," said Lottavim, and they gave each other a giant hug.

2 1982 02245 3736